24688   Jnf 567.9

j567.9
Sattler, Helen Roney.
Stegosaurs : the
solar-powered dinosaurs /
Helen Roney Sattler ;
illustrated by Turi

STEGOSAURS
THE SOLAR-POWERED DINOSAURS

First Edition 1 2 3 4 5 6 7 8 9 10

Library of Congress Cataloging in Publication Data
Sattler, Helen Roney. Stegosaurs : the solar-powered dinosaurs / by Helen Roney Sattler : illustrations by Turi MacCombie.
p.   cm.   Includes bibliographical references.   Summary: Discusses the armor-plated dinosaur called Stegosaurus and
some of its lesser-known relatives.
ISBN 0-688-10055-4—ISBN 0-688-10056-2 (lib. bdg.)   1. Stegosaurus—Juvenile literature.   [1. Stegosaurus.
2. Dinosaurs.]   I. MacCombie, Turi, ill.   II. Title.   QE862.065S37 1992 567.9'7—dc20 90-49733 CIP AC

STEGOSAURS

THE SOLAR-POWERED DINOSAURS

HELEN RONEY SATTLER

ILLUSTRATED BY TURI MacCOMBIE

LOTHROP, LEE & SHEPARD BOOKS   NEW YORK

WHERE STEGOSAURS

1. Chialingosaurus
2. Craterosaurus
3. Dacentrurus
4. Dravidosaurus
5. Huayangosaurus
6. Kentrosaurus
7. Lexovisaurus
8. Paranthodon
9. Stegosaurus
10. Tuojiangosaurus
11. Wuerhosaurus

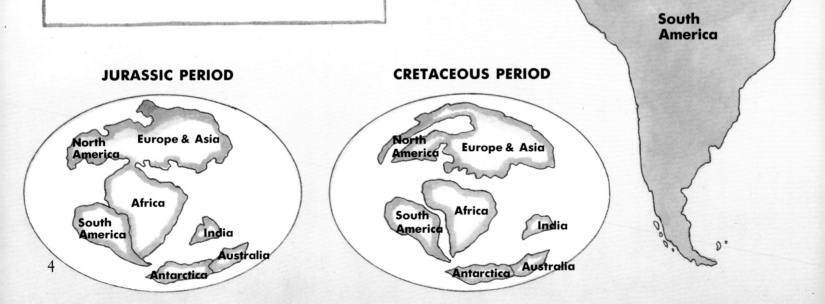

.9

.9

North America

South America

JURASSIC PERIOD

North America
Europe & Asia
Africa
South America
India
Australia
Antarctica

CRETACEOUS PERIOD

North America
Europe & Asia
South America
Africa
India
Australia
Antarctica

Poor *Stegosaurus*! People have made fun of this dinosaur for a long time, just because it was rather strange-looking and had a small brain. *Stegosaurus* (STEG-o-sawr-us) belonged to a group of dinosaurs called stegosaurs. Although *Stegosaurus* was the largest and the best known of the stegosaurs, it wasn't the only member of the group. Scientists have found fossils of ten other kinds of stegosaurs.

The stegosaurs were different from other dinosaurs. Their name means "plated lizards," and they had two rows of plates and spikes running down the middle of their backs. Stegosaurs didn't all look exactly alike. They were different sizes and had different kinds of plates, but they all had the same basic body design. They looked strange because their bodies were huge and their heads were tiny, and they carried their heads close to the ground. This was because their hind legs were more than twice as long as their forelegs.

People who make fun of stegosaurs don't realize that the stegosaurs were actually very successful animals in spite of their Ping-Pong-ball-size brains. Their fossils have been found around the world—in North America, Europe, Africa, and Asia. The stegosaurs lasted about a hundred million years, from the middle of the Jurassic period 165 million years ago to the end of the late Cretaceous period 65 million years ago. And that is a pretty impressive record for any animal group. Consider the family of the modern Asian elephant, whose body is about the same size as that of *Stegosaurus* and similar in shape. The Asian elephant has lived only 45 million years and it is already in danger of becoming extinct.

One of the reasons stegosaurs lived so long is that they adapted well to their environment. Stegosaurs carried their heads very low to the ground, and this made it easy for them to eat low-growing ground plants, such as cycads, horsetails, and fern fronds. Other plant eaters living at that time either could not or did not eat those plants.

Some people wonder how animals with such tiny heads and huge bodies could eat enough to stay alive. The head of a 16-foot-long stegosaur was only 18 inches long. However, that is only a little smaller than the head of a modern giraffe. Giraffes eat almost continually, and they eat only highly nutritious plants. Stegosaurs probably did the same thing. We know that they didn't take time to chew their food because stegosaur teeth could not be used for chewing or grinding and were weak.

The mouth of a stegosaur was equipped with a horny, turtlelike beak and chopping teeth that were used to snip off tender shoots from plants. The food was probably swallowed whole and stored in the stomach for several days while it fermented. The great size of the rib cage suggests that a stegosaur's stomach was at least as large as that of a giraffe or even an elephant, two animals that also swallow their food whole.

Stegosaurs didn't need to move fast to find plenty of food, and they weren't designed for speed. Instead, the feet of these slow-moving creatures were very strong and designed for carrying heavy loads. The front feet looked a little like an elephant's, with five short, strong toes ending in short, rounded claws. The back feet had only three toes, which were very wide.

Since stegosaurs could not run away from predators, they developed other ways to protect themselves. Scientists found fossil skeletons of many *Stegosaurus* close together in Utah and several *Kentrosaurus* (KEN-tro-sawr-us) that had been buried together in Tanzania. This suggests that at least some stegosaurs may have grazed in large herds for protection.

It was once thought that the plates running down their backs protected stegosaurs from enemies. But now we know that the plates could not have provided much protection except by making stegosaurs look larger. These bony plates were not a part of the skeleton; scientists think they were firmly embedded in the skin. No one knows for sure what the plates were for. They may have been used to attract a mate. Most scientists think that the plates acted like radiators or solar panels to control stegosaurs' body temperature. Perhaps the great amount of food fermenting in their stomachs generated a lot of heat that they needed to get rid of.

Elephants get rid of their excess heat by waving their huge ears. Giraffes lose heat through their long, slender legs and necks. Scientists believe that the stegosaur's plates did the same thing. Studies show that the plates were covered with skin and had many blood vessels running through them. Wind blowing around the plates would cool the blood and the dinosaur. On the other hand, on a cool day, sun shining on the plates would warm the blood flowing through them and give the stegosaur energy. The number and shape of the plates and their arrangement on the back were different for each kind of stegosaur. It has been suggested that those that lived in warmer climates did not need as many or as large plates as those in cooler climates.

No matter where it lived, every stegosaur had four large, horn-covered spikes (some were up to 3 feet long) near the end of its tail. These were almost certainly used for protection. They protected the stegosaur's sides and belly very well, as any crocodile or *Allosaurus* (AL-o-sawr-us) that tried to catch one soon found out. The muscles of the tail were very strong—strong enough to hold the tail well off the ground if the dinosaur wanted to. A stegosaur also could swing its tail from side to side with great force. A blow with one of the spikes to the underside of an *Allosaurus* or other large meat eater could cause great damage. Stegosaurs also had a layer of bony knobs and

11

bumps over other parts of their bodies, especially around their throats. It's easy to see why stegosaurs were around for so long. Animals with good defense systems almost always survive longer than those without good defense systems.

Stegosaurs hatched from large, oval eggs and could eat plants soon after they left their eggs. The babies looked a lot like their parents, except their heads, though still tiny, were somewhat larger (compared to their bodies) than an adult's head. Their hind legs were much longer than their forelegs. Babies had horny beaks, but they did not have plates on their backs. The plates grew in when they were older. The youngest stegosaur ever found was a baby *Stegosaurus* that was about the size of a collie dog. Although it was very young, it was not newly hatched. We don't know for sure if mother stegosaurs protected their babies, but there were fossils of several adult *Stegosaurus* near the fossils of the baby, which suggests that they might have been guarding it.

Ceratosaurus

Allosaurus

The largest *Stegosaurus* grew to be 25 to 30 feet long—longer than a school bus. They were 12 feet tall at the hips (higher than the ceiling of most classrooms) and weighed more than 4 tons (about as much as an African elephant). Some *Stegosaurus*, however, were only 15 to 20 feet long and 8½ feet tall (about the size of a pickup truck) and weighed only 2 tons.

The plates of *Stegosaurus* were thin and roughly diamond-shaped. They ran from the neck to partway down the tail. Scientists believe these plates were arranged alternately rather than in pairs and stood upright. The largest plates grew over the hip area. Some were 2 feet wide and 2 feet tall. The plates on the neck were much smaller.

Huge herds of *Stegosaurus* lived in North America during the late Jurassic period, from about 145 million years ago to 135 million years ago. Their fossils, including many complete skeletons, have been found in Colorado, Nevada, Wyoming, and Utah.

Stegosaurus probably lived in lowland areas that bordered an inland sea. The climate was semitropical, with wet and dry seasons similar to those of the African savannas. The stegosaurs may have roamed swamplands, grazing on the lush ground plants that grew there. They most likely avoided large predators such as *Allosaurus* and *Ceratosaurus* (sair-AT-o-sawr-us) by staying away from the main watering places. They had nothing to fear from the *Brachiosaurus* (BRAK-ee-o-sawr-us), *Apatosaurus* (ah-PAT-o-sawr-us), or *Camptosaurus* (KAMP-toh-sawr-us) that shared the area.

Brachiosaurus

Note: These dinosaurs are not drawn to scale.

Camptosaurus

14

Apatosaurus

The first stegosaur ever found was *Kentrosaurus*, the "spiked lizard." It lived at about the same time as *Stegosaurus* and in a similar habitat, but it lived in Africa. Its fossils were found in Tanzania. Fifty were buried together in one bed.

Kentrosaurus was only 16½ feet long (about the size of an African elephant) and weighed about 2 tons. It was shaped like *Stegosaurus*, but its plates were very different. On its neck and shoulders the plates were narrow and flat and similar in shape and size to those of *Stegosaurus*. But toward the rear of the animal they were spikelike. Eight pairs of very sharp spines ran along *Kentrosaurus*'s backbone, from the hips to the tip of its tail. Those over the hips were more than 2 feet long. In addition to this double row

15

of spines, it had another pair of spines jutting out from the back of the hips on either side. Scientists think *Kentrosaurus* may have developed spikes over its hip area to protect the large nerve section that was located there. These nerves operated the legs and tail. In a fight, *Kentrosaurus* may have turned its spiny rear toward its foe and pounded it with its spiked tail.

One of the earliest stegosaurs, *Huayangosaurus* (HWAH-YAHNG-o-sawr-us), the "Huayang lizard," lived from 162 million years ago to 150 million years ago. The fossils of this primitive stegosaur were found in mid-Jurassic deposits in the Sichuan Province of China. *Huayangosaurus* was an unusual stegosaur because it had teeth in the front of its upper jaw and its head was more square than that of most stegosaurs. *Huayangosaurus* is known from a nearly complete skeleton that is only 13½ feet long. A double row of narrow, flat plates ran down the middle of its back and halfway down its tail, except over the hips. There, the plates were replaced by two long spikes. Scutes (bony shields like those on an alligator's back) protected the sides of its body.

Another very early stegosaur, *Lexovisaurus* (leks-OH-vih-sawr-us), the "Lexovian lizard," lived in England and France 162 to 158 million years ago. This middle Jurassic stegosaur is known from several incomplete skeletons. It was quite similar to *Kentrosaurus*. The plates along the neck, shoulders, and back of *Lexovisaurus* were small, narrow, and flat. Spikes ran down its tail from the hips to the tip. A huge spike over each hip jutted toward the rear.

Dacentrurus (dah-sen-TROO-rus), "spiked tail," lived in western Europe during the late Jurassic period. Its fossils have been found in England, France, and Portugal. Scientists think that a dinosaur egg found in Portugal may have been laid by *Dacentrurus*, because its fossils were found nearby. The egg is oval and larger than a large baked potato. *Dacentrurus* had a relatively long tail, and its forelegs were longer than those of *Stegosaurus*. This stegosaur was 15 feet long. Two rows of small spikelike plates ran down its back. Its tail spikes were long and massive.

Tuojiangosaurus (twah-JEEAHNG-o-sawr-us), the "Tuojiang lizard," roamed eastern China between 152 and 140 million years ago, about the same time that *Stegosaurus* and *Kentrosaurus* browsed the swamplands of North America and Africa. *Tuojiangosaurus* is known from a nearly complete skeleton. It was 23½ feet long and 8½ feet tall at the hips—about the same size as *Stegosaurus*. Its plates, however, were quite different. It had fifteen pairs of plates running from the neck to halfway down the tail. These plates were narrower and more cone-shaped than those of *Stegosaurus*.

Chialingosaurus (chee-ah-LING-o-sawr-us), the "Chialing River lizard," also lived in China, but somewhat later than *Huayangosaurus*. This slender, 16-foot-long stegosaur had spikelike plates similar to those of *Kentrosaurus*, but they were smaller and a little more platelike. *Chialingosaurus*'s spiky plates ran from the middle of its back to the end of its tail.

It was once thought that stegosaurs did not live beyond the Jurassic period. However, we now know that there were stegosaurs roaming the interior lakes and steppes of what is now the Gobi Desert of Mongolia during the early Cretaceous period, about 125 million years ago. Fossils of *Wuerhosaurus* (woo-er-ho-SAWR-us), the "lizard from Wuerho," were found in early Cretaceous deposits in northwestern China. It lived from 125 to 110 million years ago and is known from a nearly complete skull-less skeleton. *Wuerhosaurus* was 26 feet long. Its plates were much shorter and wider than those of other stegosaurs.

Craterosaurus (kray-ter-o-SAWR-us), "bowl lizard," lived in early Cretaceous England from 115 to 105 million years ago. Too few of its fossils have been found to be able to determine what it looked like.

A small section of a jaw, which has been named *Paranthodon* (par-AN-tho-don), is believed to be from a stegosaur. This jaw was found in early Cretaceous rock in South Africa.

Dravidosaurus (dra-VID-o-sawr-us), "Dravid lizard," is the only stegosaur that we know about that lived to the end of the Mesozoic era. It was found in southern India. It looked more like *Stegosaurus* than like other stegosaurs, but it was much smaller. It was only 10 feet long, no bigger than a horse. The thin, triangular plates of Dravidosaurus ranged from 2 inches to 10 inches tall. The spikes on the end of its tail were 6 inches long and slightly curved.

At the end of the Jurassic period some of the stegosaurs died out. It was during this time that the large super-continents had begun to break apart and climates and habitats changed. Flowering plants replaced cycads and ferns. Ankylosaurs, a new kind of armored dinosaur that also fed on low ground plants, appeared on the scene. During the late Cretaceous period, ankylosaurs thrived everywhere except in India, which had separated from the African continent before ankylosaurs developed.

Some scientists think that many of the stegosaurs became extinct because they were crowded out by the ankylosaurs. The ankylosaurs were not smarter; they just ate the same low ground plants that the stegosaurs ate and there were more of them. Where there were no ankylosaurs, the stegosaurs continued to live to the end of the Mesozoic era.

Although stegosaurs weren't very pretty, there are many things to admire about them. These dinosaurs were able to survive for a very long period even though their brains were tiny. They made good use of what they had and very successfully adapted to their environments.

29

LIFE SPANS OF THE STEGOSAURS

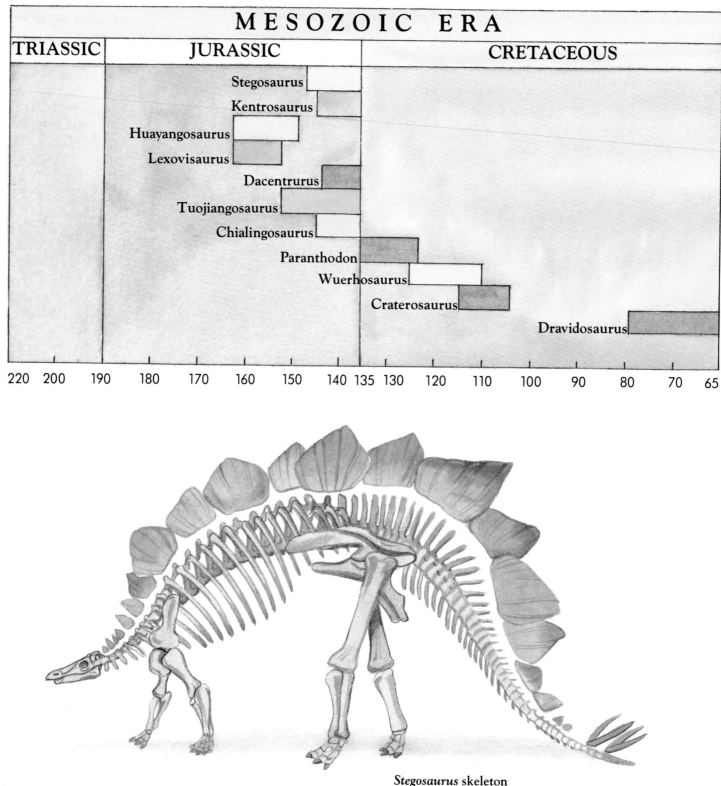

	MESOZOIC ERA	
TRIASSIC	JURASSIC	CRETACEOUS

Stegosaurus

Kentrosaurus

Huayangosaurus

Lexovisaurus

Dacentrurus

Tuojiangosaurus

Chialingosaurus

Paranthodon

Wuerhosaurus

Craterosaurus

Dravidosaurus

MILLIONS OF YEARS

220 200 190 180 170 160 150 140 135 130 120 110 100 90 80 70 65

Stegosaurus skeleton

INDEX

For Further Reading

Bakker, Robert T. *The Dinosaur Heresies*. New York: William Morrow & Co., 1986.

Benton, Michael. *The Dinosaur Encyclopedia*. New York: Mayflower Books, 1979.

Charig, Alan J. *A New Look at the Dinosaurs*. New York: Mayflower Books, 1979.

Glut, Donald F. *The New Dinosaur Dictionary*. Secaucus, N.J.: Citadel Press, 1982.

Norman, David. *The Illustrated Encyclopedia of Dinosaurs*. New York: Crescent Books, 1985.

Norman, David, and Angela Milner. *Eyewitness Books: Dinosaurs*. New York: Alfred A. Knopf, 1989.

Russell, Dale A. *An Odyssey in Time: The Dinosaurs of North America*. Minocqua, Wisc.: Northwold Press, Inc., 1989.

Sattler, Helen Roney. *The New Illustrated Dinosaur Dictionary*. New York: Lothrop, Lee & Shepard Books, 1990.

Zhiming, Dong. *Dinosaurs from China*. Beijing: China Ocean Press, 1987.